The Rat and the Tiger

Keiko Kasza

PUFFIN BOOKS

PUFFIN BOOKS
Published by the Penguin Group
Penguin Young Readers Group, 345 Hudson Street, New York, New York 10014, U.S.A.
Penguin Group (Canada), 90 Eglinton Avenue East, Suite 700, Toronto, Ontario, Canada M4P 2Y3
(a division of Pearson Penguin Canada Inc.)
Penguin Books Ltd, 80 Strand, London WC2R 0RL, England
Penguin Ireland, 25 St Stephen's Green, Dublin 2, Ireland
(a division of Penguin Books Ltd)
Penguin Group (Australia), 250 Camberwell Road, Camberwell, Victoria 3124, Australia
(a division of Pearson Australia Group Pty Ltd)
Penguin Books India Pvt Ltd, 11 Community Centre, Panchsheel Park, New Delhi - 110 017, India
Penguin Group (NZ), 67 Apollo Drive, Mairangi Bay, Auckland 1311, New Zealand
(a division of Pearson New Zealand Ltd)
Penguin Books (South Africa) (Pty) Ltd, 24 Sturdee Avenue, Rosebank, Johannesburg 2196, South Africa

Registered Offices: Penguin Books Ltd, 80 Strand, London WC2R 0RL, England

First published in the United States of America by G. P. Putnam's Sons, a division of Penguin Young Readers Group, 1993
Published by Puffin Books, a division of Penguin Young Readers Group, 2007

1 3 5 7 9 10 8 6 4 2

Text copyright © Keiko Kasza, 1993

THE LIBRARY OF CONGRESS HAS CATALOGED THE PUTNAM EDITION AS FOLLOWS:
Kasza, Keiko. The rat and the tiger / Keiko Kasza. p.   cm.
Summary: In his friendship with Rat, Tiger takes advantage and plays the bully because of his greater size,
but one day Rat stands up for his rights.
ISBN 0-399-22404-1 (hc)
[1. Rats—Fiction. 2. Tigers—Fiction. 3. Friendship—Fiction. 4. Bullies—Fiction.] I. Title.
PZ7.K15645Rat 1993 [E]—dc20 91-34413 CIP
Puffin Books ISBN 978-0-14-240900-8
Manufactured in China

To my parents

I'm a rat, just a tiny little rat.
Tiger is a big tough fellow.
We are best friends.
    We used to have a little problem, though. . . .

Whenever we played cowboys,
Tiger was always the good guy,
and I was the bad guy.

Tiger said, "The good guy always wins in the end."
What could I say? I'm just a tiny little rat.

Whenever Tiger and I shared a doughnut, Tiger always cut it so that his piece was bigger than mine.

Tiger said, "It's nice to share, isn't it?"
What could I say? I'm just a tiny little rat.

Whenever Tiger saw a flower he liked,
he just pointed and expected me
to get it for him.

Tiger said, "Isn't nature beautiful?"
What could I say? I'm just a tiny little rat.

One day I built a castle, the biggest one
I had ever made.
  "Look, Tiger!" I shouted proudly.
  Tiger said, "Nice job, Rat."

Then he jumped into the air and kicked
my castle to pieces!

"That's it, Tiger!" I screamed.
"You're not my friend anymore.
I may be a tiny little rat
but you're a big mean bully!
Good-bye!"

I was mad. And I was sad.
But most of all, I was scared.
I had never yelled at Tiger like that before.

When Tiger found me, my heart almost stopped. I thought he might kick me just like he had kicked my castle.

"Go away, Tiger!" I shouted.
"I'm not afraid of you. Leave me alone!"

But Tiger didn't come to kick me.
He had fixed my castle, and he
wanted me to see it. So I did.

But I told him, "I'm still not
your friend."

Then Tiger asked me if I wanted to play the good cowboy for a change. So I did.

But I told him, "I'm still not your friend."

Next, Tiger asked me if I wanted to cut our doughnut for once.
So I did.

But I told him, "I'm still not your friend."

Finally, Tiger asked me if I wanted a flower.
So I pointed to one, and Tiger bravely
went to pick it for me.

"Maybe," I told him, "just maybe I'll be your friend again."
Tiger smiled.

Ever since that day, we have gotten along just fine.
We take turns at everything. And we split
our doughnuts right down the middle.

    We do have a little problem, though. . . .

A new kid on the block!